Stoneywish
and other chilling stories

Stoneywish
and other chilling stories

Joan Aiken
Illustrated by Masha Ukhova

BLOOMSBURY EDUCATION
LONDON   OXFORD   NEW YORK   NEW DELHI   SYDNEY

BLOOMSBURY EDUCATION
Bloomsbury Publishing Plc
50 Bedford Square, London, WC1B 3DP, UK

BLOOMSBURY, BLOOMSBURY EDUCATION and the Diana logo
are trademarks of Bloomsbury Publishing Plc

First published in 2004 by A&C Black, an imprint of Bloomsbury Publishing Plc

This edition published in 2020 by Bloomsbury Publishing Plc

This collection © Joan Aiken Enterprises Ltd, 2004

"Stoneywish" © Joan Aiken Enterprises Ltd, 1995. "Snow Horse" © Joan Aiken Enterprises
Ltd, 1982. First published in *A Whisper in the Night* (Victor Gollancz, 1982). The Publishers
would like to thank The Random House group Ltd for permission to include "Snow Horse".
"Bindweed" © Joan Aiken Enterprises Ltd, 1989. First pubished in *A Foot in the Grave*
(Jonathan Cape, 1989). "The Road from Rushout Wood" © Joan Aiken Enterprises Ltd,
1992. First published in *Chilling Christmas Stories* (Scholastic, 1992)

Illustrations copyright © Masha Ukhova, 2020.
Cover artwork © George Ermos, 2020

Packaged for Bloomsbury by Plum5 Limited

Joan Aiken has asserted her right under the Copyright, Designs and Patents Act,
1988, to be identified as Author of this work

A catalogue record for this book is available from the British Library

ISBN: PB: 978-1-4729-6773-2;
ePDF: 978-1-4729-6772-5; ePub: 978-1-4729-6775-6

2 4 6 8 10 9 7 5 3 1

Printed and bound by CPI Group (UK) Ltd, Croydon, CR0 4YY

Contents

Stoneywish

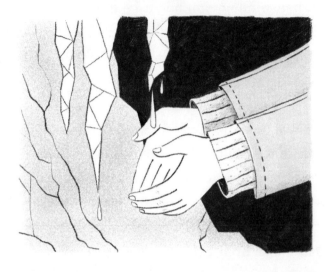

My Dad's a plumber. STONEYWISH SANITARY, it says on the side of his van. He is a solitary, silent man, likes driving about and fixing people's pipes; that way he doesn't have to do too much talking.

Stoneywish is the village where we live, half a dozen houses, pub, and church, set among a lot of huge thorn, hazel, and blackberry clumps in the middle of a rough, tussocky common five miles from Marston Wells.

It's a funny thing, in our village, none of the houses can be seen from any other; look from our kitchen window, you might be living in a wood. Perhaps that's why Dad chose to live in the place.

Three hundred years ago, Stoneywish was much bigger (Mr Lee, who teaches history, told me) but then almost all the people in it caught the plague. The County Sheriff ordered a big, high fence built all the way round the houses, and nobody was to be allowed in or out until the people had either died or got better. Most died.

Our family wasn't living here in those times. Dad came from overseas twenty years ago, his name was Xarzziq, which he changed to Chark. But I was born in Stoneywish.

On the day that I was born, Dad was driving my Mum along the winding, narrow lane that leads from Stoneywish to Marston Wells to buy wool to make a shawl. It was a misty, wintry day. And there was a fellow in a sports car behind Dad on the road who was wild to get past – he kept spurting up close, weaving and honking on his horn, twisting and swerving and shaking his fist – Dad said he felt like a cow with a gadfly on its tail, and this impatient, pestilent fellow was driving him crazy with such a carry-on, and no way to let him by, the road being so narrow and twisty, all among the blackthorn and bramble bushes.

Then – all of a sudden, rounding a big tangled clump of thorn on his left – my Dad sees somebody ahead of him on the road – a person, an old skinny fellow with a white beard, making his slow tottery way across, limping on a stick.

Of course my Dad crammed on his brake – and at that the furious fellow behind comes swooping past, with a blare on his horn, side-swiping my Dad's rear fender, so that Dad swerved violently across the road and ends up with his radiator jammed into a bramble-bush on the right-hand side.

In a moment the sports car had zipped on its way, with a roar, and was out of sight. And the old pedestrian who'd been the cause of the trouble – to Dad's amazement *he* wasn't hurt at all, but had somehow contrived to shuffle across, just before the sports car overtook – he came to help see to my Mum, who was badly shook and shocked.

"Ought to be sat in the stocks, that sort, and have rotten eggs shied at 'em," says the old man. Meaning the driver of the sports car. And, "If you'd been born in this place, friend, you could have used your Stoneywish on him."

Dad, busy comforting Mum, paid no heed to this, thought the old boy must be a bit touched in his wits. How could he know, anyway, where Dad was born?

Having managed to reverse the van out, back on to the road, and finding there was not much damage done, Dad turned round and made for home. The old man had limped off into the bushes.

Dad soon forgot all about him.

For that night I was born, and my Mum died.

I've always been lame, like you see, so my mates tease me, calling me Rickety, instead of Rick. Rickety Chark. I don't mind, not too much.

I'm going into the plumbing business, like my Dad; plumbers are always in demand. They don't need to have both legs the same length.

But that's one of the reasons why Dad is rather silent and keeps himself to himself. He misses Mum.

Now, the strange thing is this: that old man who crossed the road, my Dad never saw him again. But I have seen him, different times. And most people who live in Stoneywish *do* see him, now and again. He's known as Old Carpenter.

If you pass by Farmer Westrupp's big meadow, you'll see there's three milk bottles standing out in the middle. Morning or midday, they're always empty. But by evening-time, somebody has always filled those bottles up. And then, by next morning, they are empty again. If you ask about them, most folk won't answer. But some will say, off-hand, that they are for Old Carpenter.

Mrs Sollett told me about him. She's the widow-lady who came to housekeep for my Dad and take care of me after my Mum died. She's old, and she has always lived in the village.

"Old Carpenter's been here since plague time." she told me, when I was about four, and began asking questions.

Sometimes, when you are walking on the Common, you get a flash in the corner of your eye – just a glimpse of someone tall as a beanpole, wearing white workmen's overalls like a house-painter. Or you'll see him stooping among the tombstones in the tangled graveyard, pulling out a dock or a bunch of ragwort. Or by the brook, poking with a hazel-rod at a snarl of driftwood that's lodged against the buttress of the bridge. Or picking a ripe cob nut from the hedge. Just a quick glance at him, sidelong, is all you ever get; if you turn to look at him straight, he's gone.

"In general, it's only folk born here that can see him," Mrs Sollett told me. "I never knew someone who came from outside, like your Dad, to get a sight of him. Let alone hear him speak! That's really uncommon. My husband's grandfather used to tell us that he once heard Old Carpenter speak. But he's the only other I ever heard tell of."

"What did he say, Mrs Sollett?"

"Granddad would never tell us that."

"What did Old Carpenter mean, Mrs Sollett, about being born here? And the Stoneywish?"

"Oh," says Mrs Sollett, "it's just a tale the children tell, handed down from the old days. You'll hear it soon enough when you get to school. From that time when all the people were shut up inside the village and couldn't get out. With the plague and all. That was a bad time. I reckon things got sorta curdled and fizzy in Stoneywish then, like bottled plums when they start to go off. Things went odd, went nasty. And it's believed that every child born in the village since then gets a wish; if they live to the age of nine. The night before their ninth birthday they get the wish. And it's called a Stoneywish."

"I've still got time, then," I said. "But what's a Stoneywish, Mrs Sollett?"

"You can wish the wish for yourself, or for another person." she says.

"There's a rhyme about it:

Stoneywish, what's your will
Name it, child, for good or ill,
Stoneywish, stoney way
Never doubt, another day
Sun or storm, shine or rain
Home will come your wish again."

"What does that mean?"

"Why, they say Old Carpenter (*young* Carpenter, he would have been in those days, and he really was a carpenter, people were named by what they did, then, your Dad would have been Mister Plumber) – Carpenter had caught the plague, but got better, as a very few did. So he was given the job of building the fence, twelve foot high, all around the village. And he had to live outside the fence, in a hut, when it was done; and men came every day from the Sheriff's office, bringing food for him to throw over the fence to the folk inside. Well, it's said, the people inside were angry, that Carpenter was free and they were not, and so they wished a wish on him, that he'd always seek, and never find. And, they

say, that's why he hangs about here, to this day –
seeking, seeking, and never finding. There's
another rhyme that goes:

Wish your wish for friend or foe
The wish will follow wherever you go."

"Perhaps Old Carpenter wished a wish?" I
said. "Maybe he wished that somebody, someone
he knew, would stay alive and not die of the
plague? And then the wish came back on him?
He stayed alive, on and on?"

"Ah – maybe so. They say he was plighted
to marry a girl, Sorrell Penfold. But she was shut
up inside the village, and she was one as died of
the plague."

"Mum's name was Prue Penfold," I said.

"Ah, there's always been Penfolds at
Stoneywish. Your Mum would have been a great-
great-grand-niece of Sorrell, I dare say. Maybe
it's because he was married to Prue that your
Dad was able to see Old Carpenter that time."

As the years went by, my Dad took to thinking,
more and more, about what Old Carpenter had

said to him: "If you had been born in this place, you could have used your Stoneywish on him."

One day Dad said to me: "I'd dearly like to see that chap who hit my van get his desserts. It was all because of him that your Mum died. I'd like him to be punished."

"But, Dad, you don't know who he was! And it's seven years ago now. How could you ever trace him?"

"If you were to use your Stoneywish on him, when it comes due," said Dad, "that would trace him soon enough."

Then I saw how his thoughts were running, and that turned me cold to my backbone. Next year I'd be eight, and at the end of *that* year I'd have command of my Stoneywish.

My friend Polly, she'd turned nine the month before, so I asked her about it.

"What do you do, Polly, when you have the wish? What happens?"

"First, you have to find out the exact time of day that you were born," Polly told me. "I was born at tea-time – all my brothers and sisters were too, so that was easy. Then you have to go, all by yourself, to St Annadoc's spring."

That was a spring over on the far side of the Common, where there's a kind of a low cliff, and the water comes pouring out of a hole in the rock, and falls into a sizeable pool at the bottom. It's clear and very cold and tastes of flint.

"You go to St Annadoc's, all by yourself," says Polly, "and you take a twig of mountain ash, to keep off the bad things, and drop it in the pool. Then you drink, once, twice, three times, from the water as it trickles out, and you say,

Whether I wish for foe or friend
My wish will come back to me in the end
Here's my wish, time will tell
If it be for ill or well.

Then you wish your wish, and then you go home."

"What did you wish, Polly?"

She giggled. "You're not supposed to tell, really. But it's all over now so it can't matter. You know, they always say its best if you wish a kind

17

wish for somebody else. Then, if it comes back on you, at least it is kind. Jamie Thatcher, he wished that whoever stole his Dad's apples should break his leg; and, sure enough, young Ted Fowler had a motorbike smash, and he's still in a cast in Marstone Hospital, and they're pretty sure it was Ted took the apples; but then Jamie broke *his* leg, skating, so I reckoned that was a no-good wish. It came back on him. – So I wished that my Mum should have a treat, something that would make her happy. Dear knows, she works hard enough for us all, and never gets a single day off."

"And what happened? Did she get a treat?"

Polly giggled again. "Mum told us she's having another baby. And she's really pleased about it! So I reckon that's her treat. But what if it happens to me?"

"Don't be clung-headed," I said. "Babies only happen to grown-up ladies."

What Polly had said, though, gave me a lot to think about.

Dad kept on and on at me about the Stoneywish.

"It's your duty to your Mum," was what he kept saying.

"You couldn't even run away to sea," Dad said sourly. "They wouldn't take you. Do something useful!"

"Why can't I wish that my leg would get better! Instead of wishing harm to some long-ago stranger? Maybe he's mended his ways by now."

"He ought to suffer," Dad said obstinately, "Look at the harm he's done us."

My birthday comes in January. Snow and frost and bitter winds, chasing among the grey hoary clumps on Stoneywish Common. Christmas long gone by, and nothing to look forward to. But the weather didn't keep Old Carpenter from his usual wanderings. Indeed, at that time I saw more of him than I ever had before: on the church tower, peering down through a snow-drizzle, or by the edge of Sligo Pond where the geese slopped dolefully about on two-inch-thick ice, or listening to the bleating by Farmer Westrup's yard, where the straw-thatched pens were full of new-born lambs.

And each time that I saw Old Carpenter I thought that he gave me a look – almost a nod, almost a signal – as much as to say, "I'd talk to you if I could, I've a message to pass on to you."

Only, what message could he have for me?

Winter or no, his bottles of milk were always put out for him. Somebody always took care of that.

Of course, at this time of year, Dad was wanted everywhere. Burst water-mains, frozen pipes, cracked tanks, over-heated boilers, pipe-lagging chewed up by starving house-mice – Dad was out all day, from long before the late, gloomy sunrise till long after the last foggy blink of the red sun before it settled down among the blackberry clumps.

One thing, I thought: Dad's so busy, he's probably forgotten my birthday.

But I was wrong. Dad said: "I'm coming with you, on Saturday, when you go to that wishing-well."

"But you can't do that, Dad. A person has to go alone."

"I'm coming," Dad said obstinately, and I thought, in relief, Well that will put a stopper on the whole business. And it won't be my fault.

But the very day before my birthday, Dad's van skidded on a dreadful patch of ice on Friday Hill as he was coming home from a long day's jobs. Mr Penfold was there soon after, and pulled him clear; there was another chap helping, but he didn't wait to be thanked. The van was a write-off; and Dad was in intensive care in Marston Hospital.

Mrs Sollett took me to see him. He was all rigged up with tubes and drips and drains, looked like one of his own plumbing jobs.

Mrs Sollett tiptoed away and left us alone for a few minutes.

Dad opened one blue eye and peered at me through bristly lashes.

"Rick..." he said in a thread of a voice. "I've had a better notion... Lean closer now..."

Just as he was finishing a nurse came in and said, "No talking, Mr Chark. Talking's not allowed." And Mrs Sollett said, "When can I bring the boy again?" and the doctor said, "We'll see..."

When I was back at home my friend Polly said, "Well, it's a bit of luck that you can use your Stoneywish to wish your Dad better. That's a *good* use for a wish. And it can't do you any harm."

"That's true," I said. "But it's not what he wants."

"What does he want, then?"

"I can't tell you..."

I'd asked Mrs Sollett what time of day I was born, and she said five o'clock in the morning. A harsh time to have to go out through the scrunching frozen grass, with no moon, and a scalding wind, and no sounds for company but the hoot of owls and foxes squalling.

Mr Penfold, Polly's father, had lent me a fine big torch, and I wore my thick rubber boots and an old sheepskin-lined coat of Dad's, cut down to my size. Even so, the cold fairly numbed me before I got to the far side of the Common. And when I came to St Annadoc's pool, my rowan-twig rattled on the frozen surface of the water, and I saw that the flow from the hole in the bank-side had dwindled to a thick lumpy icicle and a slow, steady drip.

What do I do now? I wondered. Break a bit off the icicle, or hold my hand under the drip?

I held my hand under, counting up to fifty, and had a palm full of water. Drank, and held it again, and counted, and drank and counted, and drank again.

"I wish that old Carpenter may find what he is searching for and rest in peace."

I breathed out the words, very softly, just above hearing level, then tucked my freezing hand into my pocket, and started the long unhappy limping trudge back home. This way round was even worse, the wind against my face cut like a hack-saw.

And I kept thinking, Did I do right? Was that really what Dad wanted? What made him change his mind?

Then, as I plodded along, I began to notice that somebody was plodding beside me – somebody much taller, but thin, very thin, dressed in old white clothes that fluttered in the wind. Somebody who walked with a stick.

"*Did I do right?*" I asked him.

"The fence is down," he said. "Now all may pass through."

He turned and looked at me full, for the first and only time, then drifted away in a white flutter on the icy gale.

My father got better, and the insurance paid for a new van; but he doesn't work quite so hard now. He will live with Polly and me when we get married.

Children of the village still wish on their birthdays at St Annadoc's Well, but not all of their wishes seem to get granted these days. Some do, some don't.

Old Carpenter has never been seen again in Stoneywish.

Snow Horse

A pleasant place, the Forest Lodge Inn seemed as you rode up the mountain track, with its big thatched barns and stables all around, the slate-paved courtyard in front, and the solidity of the stone house itself, promising comfort and good cheer. But inside, there was a strange chill; guests could never get warm enough in bed, pile on however so many blankets they might; the wind whispered uneasily around the corners of the building, birds never nested in its eaves, and travellers who spent a night there somehow never cared to come back for another.

Summertime was different. People would come for the day, then, for the pony-trekking; McGall, the innkeeper, kept thirty ponies, sturdy little mountain beasts, and parties would be going out every morning, all summer long, over the mountains, taking their lunch with them in knapsacks and returning at night tired and cheerful; then the Forest Lodge was lively enough. But in winter, after the first snow fell, scanty at first, barely covering the grass, then thicker and thicker till Glenmarrich Pass was blocked and for months no one could come up from the town below – ah, in winter the inn was cold, grim, and silent indeed. McGall tried many times to persuade the Tourist Board to install a ski lift on Ben Marrich, but the board members were not interested in McGall's profits, they wanted to keep their tourists alive; they said there were too many cliffs and gullies on the mountain for safe skiing. So between November and March most of the ponies would go down to Loch Dune to graze in its watermeadows, where the sea winds kept the snow away; others drowsed and grew fat in the big thatched stables.

Who looked after them? Cal did, the boy who had been fished out of a snowdrift thirteen years before, a hungrily crying baby wrapped in a sheepskin jacket. Both his parents, poor young things, lay stiff and dead by him, and not a scrap of paper on them to show who they were. Nobody came forward to claim the baby, who, it turned out, was lamed from frostbite; McGall's wife, a good-natured woman, said she'd keep the child. But her own boy, Dirk, never took to the foundling, nor did his father. After Mrs McGall died of lung trouble, young Cal had a hard time of it. Still, by then he had proved his usefulness, did more than half the work in stable and yard, and as he was never paid a penny, McGall found it handy to keep him on. He ate scraps, got bawled at, was cuffed about the head a dozen times a day, and took his comfort in loving the ponies, which, under his care, shone and throve like Derby winners.

Ride them? No, he was never allowed to do that.

"With your useless leg? Forget it," said McGall. "I'll not have my stock ruined by you fooling around on them. If I see you on the back of any of my string, I'll give you such a leathering that you won't be sitting down for a month."

Cal had a humble nature. He accepted that he was not good enough to ride the ponies. Never mind! They all loved the boy who tended them. Each would turn to nuzzle him, blowing sweet warm air through his thatch of straw-yellow hair, as he limped down the stable lines.

On a gusty day in November a one-eyed traveller came riding a grey horse up Glenmarrich Pass.

McGall and Dirk had gone down with the Land-Rover to Glen Dune to buy winter supplies, for the first snows were close ahead; by now the inn was shut up for the season, and Cal was the only soul there, apart from the beasts.

The traveller dismounted halfway up the track and led his plodding grey the rest of the way; poor thing, you could see why, for it was dead lame and hobbled painfully, hanging its head as if in grief. A beautiful dark dapple-grey, it must have been a fine horse once but was now old, thin, sick, and tired; looked as if it had been ridden a long, long way, maybe from the other side of the world. And the rider, leading it gently up the rocky path, eyed it with sorrow and regret, as if he knew, only too well, what its fate would soon be and what had brought that fate about.

Reaching the inn door, the traveller knocked hard on the thick oak with the staff he carried: rap, rap! still holding his nag's reins looped over his elbow.

Cal opened the door: a small, thin, frightened boy.

"Mr. McGall's not here, sir! He went down the mountain to buy winter stores. And he told me to let nobody in. The fires are all out. And there's no food cooked."

"It's not food I need," said the traveller. "All I want is a drink. But my horse is lame and sick; he needs rest and care. And I must buy another, or hire one, for I am riding on an urgent errand to a distant place, a long way off on the other side of the mountain."

Cal gazed at the man in doubt and fright. The stranger was tall, with a grey beard; he wore a blue riding cape and a broad-brimmed hat that was pulled down low; his face was rather stern.

"Sir," Cal said, "I would like to help you but my master will beat me if I let anyone take a horse when he is not here."

"I can pay well," said the one-eyed man. "Just lead me to the stables."

Somehow, without at all meaning to, Cal found that he was leading the traveller around the corner to the stable yard and the long, thick-roofed building where the ponies rested in warmth and comfort. The one-eyed man glanced swiftly along the row and picked out a grey mountain pony that was sturdy and trim, though nothing like so handsome as his own must once have been.

"This one will serve me," said he. "I will pay your master ten gold pieces for it" – which he counted out, from a goatskin pouch. Cal's eyes nearly started from his head; he had never seen gold money before. Each coin must be worth hundreds of pounds.

"Now fetch a bucket of warm mash for my poor beast," said the traveller.

Eagerly Cal lit a brazier, heated water, put bran into the mash, and some wine too, certain that his master would not grudge it to a customer who paid so well. The sick horse was too tired to take more than a few mouthfuls, though its master fed it and gentled it himself. Then Cal rubbed it down and buckled a warm blanket around its belly.

"How will you know that he is alive, sir?"

The one-eyed man did not answer that question but said, "Here is another gold piece to pay for his board."

"It is too much, sir," objected Cal, trembling, for there was something about the stranger's voice that echoed through and through his head, like the boom of a waterfall.

"Too much? For my faithful companion?"

Cal flinched at his tone; but the man smiled.

"I can see that you are an honest boy. What is your name?"

"Cal, sir."

"Look after my horse kindly, Cal. Now I must be on my way, for time presses. But first bring me a drink of mead."

Cal ran into the house and came back with the inn's largest beaker brimful of homemade mead, which was powerful as the midsummer sun. The traveller, who had been murmuring words of parting to his horse, drank off the mead in one gulp, then kissed his steed on its soft grey nose.

"Farewell, old friend. We shall meet in another world, if not in this."

He flung a leg over the fresh pony, shook up the reins, and galloped swiftly away into the thick of a dark cloud that hung in the head of the pass.

His own horse lifted up its drooping head and let out one piercing cry of sorrow that echoed far beyond the inn buildings.

McGall, driving back up the valley with a load of stores, heard the cry. "What the deuce was that?" he said. "I hope that lame layabout has not been up to mischief."

"Stealing a ride when he shouldn't?" suggested Dirk as the Land-Rover bounced into the stable yard.

Of course McGall was angry, very angry indeed, when he found that a useful weight-carrying grey pony was gone from his stable, in exchange for a sad, sick beast with hardly more flesh on its bones than a skeleton.

Cal made haste to give him the eleven gold coins, and he stared at them hard, bit them, tested them over a candle, and demanded a description of the stranger.

"A one-eyed fellow with a broad-brimmed hat and blue cape? Nobody from these parts. Didn't give his name? Probably an escaped convict. What sort of payment is that? I've never seen such coins. How dare you let that thief make off with one of my best hacks?"

Cal was rewarded by a stunning blow on each side of the head and a shower of kicks.

"Now I have to go down into town again to show these coins to the bank, and it's all your fault, you little no-good. And I'm not giving stable room and good fodder to that spavined wreck. It can go out in the bothy. And strip that blanket off it!"

The bothy was a miserable tumbledown shed, open on two sides to the weather. Cal dared not argue with his master – that would only have earned him another beating or a tooth knocked out – but he did his best to shelter the sick horse with bales of straw, and he strapped on it the tattered moth-eaten cover from his own bed. Forbidden to feed the beast, he took it his own meals, and he huddled beside it at night, to give it the warmth of his own body. But the grey would eat little and drink only a few mouthfuls of water. And after three days it died, from grieving for its master, Cal thought, rather than sickness.

"Good riddance," said the innkeeper, who by that time had taken the gold pieces to the bank and been told that they were worth an amazing amount of money. He kicked the grey horse's carcass. "That's too skinny to use even for dogmeat. Bury it under the stable muck in the corner; it will do to fertilize the crops next summer."

"But," said Cal, "its owner told me, if it died, to bury it under a rowan tree."

"Get out of my sight! Bury it under a rowan – what next? Go and muck out the stables, before I give you a taste of my boot."

So the body of the grey horse was laid under a great pile of straw and stable sweepings. But before this, Cal took three hairs from its mane. One he tied around his wrist, the other two he folded in a paper and kept always in his pocket.

A year went by, and the one-eyed traveller never returned to inquire after his horse.

He must have known that it died, thought Cal.

"I knew he'd never come back," said McGall. "Ten to one those coins were stolen. It's lucky I changed them right away."

When spring came, the heap of stable sweepings was carted out and spread over the steep mountain pastures. There, at the bottom of the pile, lay the bones of the dead horse, and they had turned black and glistening as coal. Cal managed to smuggle them away, and he buried them, at night, under a rowan tree.

That autumn, snow fell early, with bitter, scouring winds, so that from September onward no more travellers took the steep track up to the Forest Lodge. McGall grew surlier than ever, thinking of the beasts to feed and no money coming in; he cursed Cal for the slightest and kept him hard at work leading the ponies around the yard to exercise them.

"Lead them, don't ride them!" shouted McGall. "Don't let me see you on the backs of any of those ponies, you useless idiot! Why the deuce didn't you die in the blizzard with your wretched parents?"

Secretly Cal did not see why his lame leg should prevent his being able to sit on a horse. Night after night he dreamed of riding the mounts that he tended with such care: the black, piebald, roan, bay, grey, chestnut; when they turned to greet him as he brought their feed he would hug them and murmur, "Ah, you'd carry me, wouldn't you, if I was allowed?" In his dreams a splendid horse, fiery, swift, obedient to his lightest touch, would carry him over the mountain wherever he wanted to go.

When winter set in, only six ponies were left in the stable; the rest had been taken down to the lowland pasture. But now a series of accidents reduced these remaining: the black threw McGall when he was out searching for a lost sheep and galloped into a gully and broke its neck; the chestnut escaped from Dirk as he was tightening its shoe in the smithy and ran out on to the mountain and was seen no more; the roan and grey fell sick and lay with heaving sides and closed eyes, refusing to eat, until they died. Cal grieved for them sadly.

And, day after day, snow fell, until a ten-foot drift lay piled against the yard gate. The inmates of Forest Lodge had little to do; Cal's care of the two remaining ponies took only an hour or two each day. Dirk sulked indoors by the fire; McGall, angry and silent, drank more and more mead. Quarrelsome with drink, he continually abused Cal.

"Find something useful to do! Shovel the snow out of the front yard; suppose a traveller came by; how could he find the door? Get outside, and don't let me see your face till suppertime."

Cal knew that no traveller would come, but he was glad to get outside, and took broom and shovel to the front yard. Here the wind, raking over the mountain, had turned the snow hard as marble. It was too hard to shift with a broom; Cal had to dig it away in blocks. These he piled up on the slope outside the yard, until he had an enormous rugged mound. At last a way was cut to the front door – supposing that any foolhardy wayfarer should brave the hills in such weather.

Knowing that if he went back indoors McGall would only find some other pointless task, Cal used the blade of his shovel to carve the pile of frozen snow into the rough shape of a horse.

Who should know better than he how a horse was shaped? He gave it a broad chest, a small proud head pulled back alertly on the strong neck, and a well-muscled rump. The legs were a problem, for snow legs might not be strong enough to support the massive body he had made, so he left the horse rising out of a block of snow and carved the suggestion of four legs on each side of the block. And he made a snow saddle, but no bridle or stirrups.

"There now!" He patted his creation affectionately. "When we are all asleep, you can gallop off into the dark and find that one-eyed traveller, and tell him that I cared for his grey as well as I could, but I think its heart broke when his master left it."

The front door opened and Dirk put his head out.

"Come in, no-good," he yelled, "and peel the spuds for supper!"

Then he saw the snow horse and burst into a rude laugh.

"Mustn't ride the stock, so he makes himself a snow horsie. Bye, bye, baby boy, ride nice snow horsie, then!" He walked round the statue and laughed even louder. "Why, it has *eight legs*! Who in the world ever heard of a horse with eight legs? Dad! Dad, come out here and see what Useless has been doing!"

He stared angrily at Cal's carved horse.

"Is that how you've been wasting your time? Get inside, fool, and make the meal!"

Then smoke began to drift around the corner, and a loud sound of crackling.

"Lord above, Dad, you've gone and set fire to the stable!" cried Dirk.

Aghast, they all raced round to the stable block, which was burning fiercely.

What water they had, in tubs or barrels, was frozen hard; there was no possible way to put out the blaze. Cal did manage to rescue the bay horse, but the piebald, which was old, had breathed too much smoke, and staggered and fell back into the fire; and the bay, terrified of the flames, snapped the halter with which it had been tethered in the cowshed and ran away over the mountain and was lost.

The whole stable block was soon reduced to a black shell; if the wind had not blown the flames in the other direction, the inn would have burned too.

McGall, in rage and despair, turned on Cal.

"This is your fault, you little rat!"

"Why, master," said Cal, dumbfounded, "I wasn't even there!"

"You bring nothing but bad luck! First my wife died, now I haven't a horse left, and my stable's ashes. Get out! I never want to see your face again!"

"But – master – how can I go? It's nearly dark – it's starting to snow again..."

"Why should I care? You can't stay here. You made yourself a snow horse," said McGall, "you can ride away on that – ride it over a cliff, and that'll be good riddance."

He stamped off indoors. Dirk, pausing only to shout mockingly, "Ride the snow horsie, baby boy!" followed him, slamming and bolting the door behind him.

Cal turned away. What could he do? The wind was rising; long ribbons of snow came flying on its wings. The stable was burned; he could not shelter there. His heart was heavy at the thought of all the horses he had cared for, gone now. With slow steps he moved across the yard to the massive snow horse and laid an arm over its freezing shoulder.

"You are the only one I have left now," he told it. And he took off his wrist the long hair from the mane of the traveller's grey and tied the hair around the snow horse's neck. Then, piling himself blocks of snow for a mounting block, since this was no pony but a full-sized horse, he clambered up on to its back.

Dusk had fallen; the inn could no longer be seen. Indeed, he could hardly make out the white form under him. He could feel its utter cold, though, striking up all through his own body – and, with the cold, a feeling of tremendous power, like that of the wind itself. Then – after a moment – he could feel the snow horse begin to move and tingle with aliveness, with a cold wild thrilling life of its own. He could feel its eight legs begin to stamp and stretch and strike the ground.

Then they began to gallop.

When McGall rose next morning, sober and bloodshot-eyed and rather ashamed of himself, the very first thing he did was to open the front door.

More snow had fallen during the night; the path Cal had dug to the gate yesterday was filled in again, nine inches deep.

A line of footprints led through this new snow to the inn door – led right up to the door, as if somebody had walked to the doorstep and stood there without moving for a long time, thinking or listening.

"That's mighty strange," said McGall, scratching his head. "Someone must have come to the door – but he never knocked, or we'd have heard him. He never came in. Where the devil did he go?"

For there was only one line of footprints. None led off again.

"He was a big fellow too," said McGall. "That print is half as long again as my foot. Where did the fellow go? Where did he come from? I don't like it."

But how the visitor had come, how he had gone, remained a mystery. As for Cal, he was gone too, and the snow horse with him. Where it had stood there was only a rough bare patch, already covered by new snow.

Bindweed

It was when I was cleaning the dining-room windows that I first saw Aunt Lily, or thought I did. After she was dead, I mean. You know how, when you stand outside a window and rub off the white smears of window-clean fluid, by the time the glass is really shining and clear it acts as a mirror. You can see the sky behind you, quite dazzling; trees and buildings and the ground go dark, like a photographic transparency. It was our garden that I could see reflected, with the big walnut tree and the stretch of lawn, and a bit of the valley beyond, and a cloudy white sky; then, across this scene, carrying a white parasol, strolled our Aunt Lily, who had been dead for a year.

I was so startled that I dropped the container of Busy-BMart window cleaner and made a big pink splash all over the nasturtiums.

"Alan! Now look what you've done!" scolded Mum, passing by. It was a Saturday morning. I was earning five pounds to go bowling in the afternoon with Sandy Swithinbank. Cleaning all the downstairs windows, inside and out, double-glazing included, is a hard-earned five pounds, I can tell you. Specially with Aunt Lily thrown in.

I picked up the plastic container and, when Mum had gone on her way, peered warily back into the spotless glass of the window I had just polished. The trees hung idle and dark, the grass was bright green, with my brother Claud mowing it over in the far left-hand corner; everything was just as it should be, except that Claud would have to hurry if he was to get the grass cut before the rain came; there was a big mass of thunder-cloud piling up behind St Ebb's steeple.

No sign of Aunt Lily.

It was simply imagination, I thought with huge relief. Optical illusion. A trick of the eye. Something close at hand – a floating dandelion puff, maybe – had taken the shape of Aunt Lily's white parasol (which I knew Mum had gladly hurried off to Oxfam a week after the funeral – all Aunt Lily's belongings had flown from the house like meteorites the minute she quit it herself; nobody had wished to be reminded of her one minute longer than necessary). The notion of Aunt Lily's parasol had conjured up the old monster herself. You hear a zoom and see a vapour-trail and you think you see the plane itself. Something like that.

I thought no more of the matter, finished the windows, just before the downpour, collected my five quid from Mum and spent the afternoon bowling with Sandy, bringing him back afterwards for supper, which was Indian takeaway.

The thunderstorm, which had muttered and circled around, and gone away, and come back, all afternoon, was now well into its stride. In fact Sandy and I got properly soaked, cycling back from the bowling-rink at Portsbourne; he came up to my bedroom to dry off and borrow a pair of jeans and a T-shirt.

While we were drying our hair a tremendous flash of violet-coloured lightning made all the lights go out for a moment and illuminated the garden outside my window – the creeper and walnut tree shone a sinister livid green.

"That's funny," I heard Sandy say, as we waited for the shattering peal of thunder that followed.

"What's funny?"

He was glancing towards the window and I didn't catch his reply, which was drowned in the rumpus; it sounded as if giant babies were hurling about mammoth building blocks in the sky above us.

He didn't answer, so I repeated my question when the row had died down and the lights had come on, rather flickeringly.

"Oh, nothing. Just a crazy notion I had."

He was rather silent even after we went downstairs and started on the potato chahkee and mutton dopiaza and onion bhajis.

By and by Claud came in, irritated because the Allington golfcourse had been submerged under a flash flood and the tournament he was due to play in had been put off. My brother Claud has won a whole lot of golf trophies, silver ones. They stand on brackets all over the house. I suppose somebody has to play golf – plenty of people apparently *do* – but I've never yet met a golf player that I liked. My brother Claud is no exception. Even good-natured Sandy agrees that he is a pill.

Now he began putting us down because of our vulgar habits.

"Only erks ride pushbikes and go bowling."

"Erk yourself," I said huffily. "Golf is just a snobs' game."

At that moment a searing glare of lightning cut out all the lights once more.

"Oh dear," said Mum as we sat in the semi-darkness. "How long will they be off this time, I wonder? I want to watch *Catch 'Em Alive* at nine."

As the thunder let off yet another salvo, close at hand, something clanged in the house.

"What in the world was that?" cried Mum. "Sounded as if a coal scuttle fell down."

"Coal scuttles don't fall down, Mother dear," said Claud patiently. "Coal scuttles are down already."

Claud is always snubbing Mother and Dad in the same way that he used to put down Aunt Lily every time she opened her mouth. He excels at the art of humiliating people; he could probably make a career out of it. He is also quite a hand at practical jokes – scattering a teaspoonful of sand in your muesli while you aren't looking, or putting on the speed of the record player from 33 to 45 just before Mum plays her favourite LP. The history teacher at Markham School, Mr Jevons, suffered from a severe breakdown and had to take a term's leave of absence when he was Claud's form master. Of course that was a couple of years ago. Claud is in the Sixth now, and acts as if he were the Lord Chief Archangel; but his nature is still the same.

The lights came on again and Dad stumped in, knocking the rain off his hair.

"Blasted weather!" he said. "Just when I wanted to get to work on the bindweed. If I don't get it dug up this weekend, the whole garden will be covered with the stuff. I've never known such a year for it."

Bindweed is that creeping stuff, wild convolvulus; it has rather pretty pink-and-white flowers, but it's real murder in the garden; climbs over everything, and the roots go down to Australia. They are fragile thin white brittle things: pull at them and they all break off. You have to dig down, sometimes about four feet, ever so carefully, to get them all out; and you never *do* get them all out. Dad really hates the stuff.

"Lilies," the old country men in the village call bindweed, "they botherin' lilies."

"Why don't you use weedkiller?" said Mum as she always does.

"Because of the birds," said Dad, as *he* always does.

Claud threw up his eyes, for patience.

"One of your golf cups fell down, Claud," said Dad, helping himself to mutton and catching Claud's expression. "It's rolling around in the front hall."

"*That's* what the clang was," said Mum.

Claud bustled out, looking annoyed, and we heard him set the cup back on its bracket. Then we heard him give an odd kind of grunt, before he reappeared in the kitchen, slightly paler than usual.

"What's up?" said Mum. "You sickening for something?"

But he shook his head and said he was going upstairs to sort out his stamps. That's another thing he does: corresponds with fellow stamp-collectors all over the world.

Three minutes later he was back down, looking very mad indeed.

"Who's been in my room, messing about with my stamps?"

He glared at me and Sandy.

We said truthfully that we hadn't been near his room, and Mum confirmed this.

"Well, somebody has, and my stamps are all wet – some of them ruined, very likely."

"You probably left your window open." Mum wasn't very sympathetic. "Now, you lot, hurry up and finish, I want to get the dishes done."

As we dried the cups, she said, "Just think – it's the anniversary of Aunt Lily's death. Remember all the plates she used to break, by putting them in the rack at an angle, so they fell through? And how cross she used to get, and say it was our fault for having a plate-rack that was too big."

We began happily remembering other things about Aunt Lily: how her eyes used to dart round the table, furtively, to make sure no other member of the family had a bigger helping than hers; how she used to fuss if her pension cheque didn't arrive on the first of the month, by the first post, and would get Mum to phone the building society; how her bedroom table and window sill were completely covered with little bottles and jars that she referred to as "the remedies". How her money, pinned inside her corsets was "the wealth". How she gave off a potent reek of liquorice allsorts and how, after her death, we found a huge tin cashbox, stuffed with them, under her bed.

Aunt Lily, Father's elder brother's wife, had nagged Uncle Tom to death – or so Father always says – until he fell out of his bedroom window, or jumped out. Then Aunt Lily, having got through Uncle Tom's savings, was obliged to come and live with us.

Claud hated her worst, but we all found her a trial.

"I do want to pull my weight in the household," she was always saying. "I do want to be one of the family."

But – bar drying a plate or two, and breaking many more – she never actually did anything useful about the place, housework or shopping or assistance with cooking or cleaning. She appeared, promptly enough, for meals, and bundled off to her room pretty smartly after them again, saying that she was very tired, and had to lie down.

If it was fine, she'd sit in the garden with her old white parasol. Indeed, all summer long she wore white clothes, droopy old things that looked as if they had come from some jumble sale. "She thinks she's Miss Havisham," snarled Claud. If Mum had hung out laundry on the line, Aunt Lily would fiddle about with it, turning things round; "I'm helping your mother," she'd say with a saintly air. She might pull off a few rose-heads, not cutting down to the main stalk, where it would be some use, but just tweaking off the dead flower, so someone would have to go round after her, doing it over again; or she'd snap off the leaves of a few weeds, not rooting them up, just breaking the stalks.

"*Don't* do that, Lily," Father would say, time and again. "It only makes them sprout thicker, don't you see? They have to be dug up with a *fork.* I'll fetch you one from the tool-shed if you like."

"Oh, no, thank you, Edward dear. That would be too much for my poor heart. I have to be careful. But I do like to do my little bit; if I pull off the bindweed flowers, that will stop them from seeding. And it makes the garden took just a little tidier."

"They don't *seed*, they spread by *rooting*," Father ground through his teeth, but she never listened.

Claud took no stock in the tales about Aunt Lily's poor heart. "I bet it's just indigestion because of the way she gobbles her food."

Claud had a running battle with Aunt Lily about toast. It was his job to make the toast for breakfast, and he always put Lily's piece at the bottom of the pile, to get soft and flabby. If it was scrambled egg, he'd pour the scrambled-egg liquid all over her toast beforehand, to make it thoroughly damp.

"*I don't like soggy toast!*" she'd hiss at him furiously through her dentures, chomping away on the sodden stuff, and Claud would put on his most innocent air, and answer every time, "Oh, don't you, Aunt Lily? But I specially made it that way for you. I thought you liked your toast to be as soft as possible. I really thought so!"

She'd glare daggers at him but, because Claud is fair and handsome, and looks very like what Father's brother Tom did when he was young, she could never bring herself to be unduly nasty to him. Whereas with the rest of us she could be really sharp.

"Don't you speak to me like that, young man! You just wait till you are sixty! Then you won't think it such a joke to laugh at a poor old lady!"

Having her in the house was like permanent wet weather. Very depressing. But we all supposed we were stuck with her for years and years; despite the talk about her poor heart she seemed in superb general health and never caught so much as a cold.

Then, one evening, just a year ago, there was a power failure. (Later we heard that the cause was Sandy Swithinbank's father who, with

Sandy's help, had been lopping a rotten branch off the huge, half-dead wild cherry that grows at the bottom of his garden. The branch fell on the power line and cut off the current from half the village for nine hours.)

So there we were, groping about the house with candles and oil lamps.

Claud, who was still sore from a set-to he'd had with Aunt Lily about Sunday TV programmes – *Songs of Worship* conflicted with *Comanche Trail* and, of course, being an "old lady" and our guest, she had to have her choice – saw in this situation a chance to get a bit of his own back.

He tiptoed up astern of Aunt Lily on the upstairs landing, as she was cautiously feeling her way from the bathroom to her bedroom door, and suddenly grabbed her from behind, saying, "Boo!"

She let out the most extraordinary gasping wail, like a punctured balloon.

"Ah-h-h-h-h-h!" I heard it through my bedroom door, which was open, and doubled up laughing – it was an incredibly funny sound. Still makes me laugh to remember.

Then she sank to the floor. "Like a stick of boiled rhubarb," as Claud said.

"Oh – Aunt Lily! Is that *you?*" he cried, in pretended dismay. "I'm so very sorry! I thought it was Alan. Here, take my arm."

All kindness and solicitude, he hoisted her up and led her to her bed, where he helped her lie down and covered her with one of her old camphor-smelling shawls. Then, gasping with suppressed laughter, he came to our room.

"Did you hear her? *That'll* teach the old so-and-so to grumble because Dad has six mushrooms on his plate and she has only five!"

For once, I and my brother saw eye to eye. Both of us thought that Aunt Lily had richly deserved her fright.

After a while, the electricity came on again and we all resumed what we had been doing before; no one gave Aunt Lily another thought until Father, going up to bed at midnight, noticed that her bedroom light was still shining under her door, so tapped and looked in to see if she was all right, and found her cold and dead in her bed.

It seemed that the talk about her poor old heart had not been a lot of eyewash after all.

She was cremated, by the wish expressed in her will (which left £162, all her worldly wealth, to Father) and the ashes were scattered in our garden, also by her wish.

"I *suppose* they will be good for the ground," Father said rather gloomily, as the fine, surprisingly heavy white stuff lay about on the lily-of-the-valley leaves under the big walnut tree. Unfortunately it was a dry month, and the ashes continued to lie there day after day, embarrassingly reminding us of our deceased aunt, and the embarrassing way she had died.

Nobody blamed Claud; no one spoke of it; but he went about very subdued, not at all his usual self, for quite a number of weeks. At last, of course, he recovered, and was worse than before. Perhaps the practical benefits of what he had done suddenly struck him: Aunt Lily removed, he got back the use of his own room (he'd had to share with me while she lived in the house), so, in fact, his evil deed had really paid off.

Not – of course – that he had meant to *kill* the old girl.

Anyway, after a month it rained, her ashes washed down into the soil, and we all forgot about her; apart from my recent imagined glimpse reflected in the window, and Mother's musing remark over the drying-up: "Just think, it's the anniversary of Aunt Lily's death."

"Funny you should have remembered Aunt Lily," observed Dad, wiping the last glass and putting it on the shelf with the others. "Just now, in the front hall, when there was that big flash of lightning, I could have sworn I saw her, in that old white dress of hers, standing outside the glass panes of the front door."

"Must have been the white lightning," Mother suggested.

"I expect so. Hark at that blessed rain! The bindweed will be growing an inch an hour," Dad grumbled. "It's absolutely smothering the lilies under the walnut tree. And now it's started up in the rosebed alongside the house. The rain had better stop by tomorrow, that's all I can say."

The third step in our staircase tends to crack like a rifle-shot when somebody steps on it. We heard that noise after Father spoke. Sandy, who was sitting opposite the open door into the front hall, suddenly drew in a sharp breath, as if he had toothache.

"Is that you, Claud?" called Mother. "If you're going up, could you fetch my knitting bag? It's on the bookcase in my bedroom."

There was no answer.

"It couldn't have been Claud," I said. "Claud is upstairs already."

"That's funny."

Mother went out into the hall, carrying a lamp.

"Claud?" she called. Still there was no answer, so she ran up and fetched her own knitting. Claud could be deaf as a post to other people's requests when he chose, and he generally did choose.

"The sudden humidity is probably making the floorboards warp," Dad said when Mother came back. "But surely you can't see to knit in this light?"

"I don't have to see when I knit. Can you put me on a record, Alan?"

"No power," I reminded her.

"Oh, bother! Nor there is."

There came a slight lull in the rain, and Sandy said he thought he'd go home. He was rather quiet and glum, and I couldn't blame him. The house felt strangely cheerless, and not only because of the dim yellow lamplight. Something murky and hostile seemed to be close around us in the sultry dense night.

"I'll bring your jeans back tomorrow – or the next day," Sandy said, glancing warily about the garden as he mounted his bike and switched on the light. "So long – see you –" and he was off down the path like a *Tour de France* contestant. And I was back inside at the same speed because, idiotically, improbably, through the drips of rain from the sodden trees, I could have sworn that I heard Aunt Lily's thin, complaining whiny voice call, "Claud! Claud! Come here, Claud, I want you."

I hurled myself inside, slamming and locking the front door, and, thank goodness, at that moment, all the lights came on. I heard Mother's and Father's voices from the kitchen, raised in cheerful relief. The dazzling light made my previous thoughts seem even crazier. Just the same, something prompted me to go upstairs. The third step was silent this time – it always is, if somebody else has just stepped on it. I went to Claud's door and banged on it.

"Hey, Claud? Are you in there? Can I – can I borrow your Latin dictionary? I left mine at school."

Claud didn't answer, so I opened the bedroom door. The first thing I noticed was his window, flung wide open, with a pool of rainwater on the sill.

Then I saw the soles of his feet.

They were *outside* the window.

Upside down.

"Dad – *Dad!*" I yelled – hysterically I expect – and dashed across the room to the window. The dark outside seemed even more opaque because of the lights having just come on. I could dimly see that Claud appeared to be hanging head down, just below the window; but not what held him there.

Luckily at that moment Father arrived, could hardly believe what he saw, but took command in a practical way.

"Grab his ankles – hold them – don't let him go! – while I fetch a ladder."

So I clung for dear life on to Claud's ankles while, in about three minutes flat, Father got the ladder from the garage and leant it up against the wall by Claud's window. Between us – Mother was in the room too, by now, helping me to hold Claud – we got him undone from a thick tangle of coiled and twisted plant tendrils that was wrapped all over him. Judging by the mass of stuff, you would have thought he'd hung there for days, for weeks. I got out my penknife and was cutting through the stems; Mother sawed away with a kitchen carver. Then she ran down to the garden and helped Dad lower my brother gingerly to the ground, among all the leaves and entwined stalks and squashed white flowers.

The plant had grown up the side of the house in a huge matted mass, like ivy.

"It's *bindweed*," said Father, in a tone of total disbelief.

"But poor, poor Claud!" Mother was crying. "Is he alive?"

"His heart's still beating," said Father, feeling it.

We carried him indoors and, while we waited for the doctor's arrival, gave Claud artificial respiration, and pulled armfuls of bindweed loose from him. His face was dark and congested, but he was still breathing – just.

Another five minutes in that position, said the doctor, and he wouldn't have been – and how, in heaven's name, had he *got* into that position?

Needless to say, the doctor wouldn't accept any of our accounts of what had happened. Or, at least, he wouldn't have, he said, if he hadn't been acquainted with old Aunt Lily; but he could believe anything, he admitted, of that old harridan. And he gave Claud a massive injection, to put him to sleep for twelve hours, and recommended that somebody should sleep in his room with him.

"Just in case the bindweed climbs in through the window."

But it didn't. It seemed that Aunt Lily had shot her bolt.

Next day Father went out with a set face and a big can of Slaughterweed and painted the poison over every bindweed stem in the garden. Very soon they began to shrivel up and turn black.

"The birds must take their chance," said Father.

Claud remained thin, white, and silent for weeks after. Months. He said he couldn't remember a single thing that had happened, except he had a notion he'd heard Aunt Lily grumbling about something.

By and by he went off to university, and now seems quite a changed character; but, personally, I doubt if the change will last.

I asked Sandy, when he brought back my jeans, why he had left our house so fast.

"Because I saw the old girl," he said. "From the kitchen. I thought I must be going off my chump. I saw her come in the front door and go up the stairs."

"She must have gone into Claud's room and tipped him out of the window. Maybe that was what she did to her old man."

"Maybe he gave her soggy toast too," said Sandy.

The Road from Rushout Wood

On a frosty Christmas Eve in the early years of this century, it was the misfortune of Hugh Tregear, a young gentleman making his way across country on a bicycle, to knock his front wheel against a rock that lay in the road with such force as to render the bicycle temporarily unfit for further travel. The rim of the wheel was bent out of shape, and a blacksmith would be required, or at least a handyman with better tools at his disposal than our young traveller had about him.

Hugh, a student at the University of Cambridge, was planning to spend the Christmas holiday with his sister. Recently married to a clergyman, she had taken up residence in a small village lying some fifty miles to the east, in a part of the country unfamiliar to our young friend, who had accordingly plotted out his itinerary on a map. Consulting this in the fading light, he now found that his nearest hope of assistance appeared to lie in the village of Goose Acre, some two miles ahead of him.

Kicking aside the rock that had done the mischief, and muttering a few uncomplimentary comments about the elders of a parish who permitted their byways to remain in such a state of disuse and neglect, Hugh began lugging his bicycle as best he could along the rutted and stony lane. This task was rendered even more difficult because the forewheel refused to turn at all, and so the whole front portion of the bicycle had to be hoisted into the air. Our traveller was further burdened with a pack on his back, which contained Christmas presents as well as his toilet articles and change of clothes, so that his progress along the lane was necessarily very slow.

Many times he stopped and mopped his brow, despite the white frost that furred the leaves and thorns in the hedgerows. Many times he was tempted to leave his machine behind the hedge, in hopes of discovering some accommodating person at the next village who might be prepared to come back for it with a horse and cart. But then he recollected that it was, after all, Christmas Eve, and that most of the villagers would, by now, have left their work for the day. He guessed therefore that they might be reluctant to set out again on such a chill, gloomy, and foggy evening. Indeed, he began to wonder if there would be any chance at all of getting his machine repaired at such an hour, on such a day. The prospect of reaching his sister's house in time for any Christmas celebrations began to recede farther and farther into the doubtful distance.

Fortunately for Hugh, this part of the country was at least very flat, and he had no troublesome slopes to contend with. In fact, after traversing a mile or so of scrubby woodland (he recalled that, on the map, this coppice had been named Rushout Wood) the lane began to descend very gradually into a gentle dip, while its banks on either hand rose higher. Our traveller now thought he began to detect the vague outlines of buildings which stood back at some distance on either side of the road ahead, though in the dusk, which was now thickening fast, it was hard to be sure of this.

"It can't be a village," he thought. "Goose Acre must be still at least a mile ahead. But perhaps it may be a large farm with buildings on both sides of the track. And at a farm – especially one of such a size as this seems to be – it is certain they will have tools for mending farm machinery, and perhaps they may be able to help me straighten out my wheel. Though it is odd that I don't remember seeing a farm marked at this point on the map, I suppose I must have missed it in the dim light."

"Phew! I certainly shall be glad when I can stop dragging this heavy bike along."

Before the mishap, he had already been riding for a couple of hours. The encounter with the rock had thrown him to the ground and jarred his shoulder. He began to find himself very weary.

"If the farm people can't mend the wheel for me," he thought hopefully, "at least they might offer to put me up for the night."

And his fancy began to play with agreeable visions of a huge open farm fireplace, thick clusters of glistening berried holly over the mantel, leaping flames, mugs of hot sweet punch, and the cheerful rumble of friendly rustic conversation.

Greatly to his dismay and discouragement, what he now began to hear instead was the distant, angry barking of dogs; more than one dog, Hugh thought – two or three at the very least. Perhaps more. The baying, interspersed with howls and snarls, had a decided note of menace about it. This was not simply the straightforward watchdog alarm signal which warns the householder that a stranger's step is approaching his boundary; these sounds contained a rasping, raging, rattling reverberation which suggested, rather, a savage longing to get at the invader and tear him to pieces.

He stood still, set down the front wheel of the bicycle, and considered, looking about him in the frosty gloom.

The barking ahead of him intensified in volume. There began to be something positively hysterical, frenzied, in its tone.

How many dogs could they have at this farm, for Heaven's sake? And on which side of the road was their territory? And were they tied up or loose?

At this juncture Hugh began to debate in his mind whether it would not be better to turn back. He was no coward, and could have dealt well enough, he told himself, with *one* dog, even if it came at him with hostile intent – but if there were two, or three, or four...? His tweed jacket and thin flannel trousers would be wholly insufficient protection against their fangs (and now he could not repress a sharp shudder at the prospect of sharp, dirty teeth gouging into his neck and arms and legs), and he had no weapon with which to defend himself.

Hesitating, he glanced back along the lane, which ran straight as a rule, sloping gently upwards out of the little dell. He tried to recall how great a distance lay between the last village he had passed and the point where his accident had taken place. A mile? Two miles? And he had pushed the bike for at least a mile through the wood. That meant probably three miles before he got back to the village – a grubby, depressed little hamlet called Cropham, where he had briefly considered trying to obtain a cup of tea at one of the cottages before deciding that they all looked too dirty and unpromising. No, there was little to be hoped for from Cropham. And yet, Hugh thought, he had really better turn back.

The baying of the dogs ahead of him was now positively bloodcurdling. But when Hugh looked more carefully along the lane towards Rushout Wood, what he saw there changed his attitude so completely that, regardless of what peril lay ahead, nothing in the world would have made him return along the way that he had come. Any danger from the dogs suddenly seemed a minor consideration.

Rushout Wood itself was now no more than a black mass of furry trees that spread out like a wolf's pelt across the horizon.

Out of the trees, and along the narrow straight road, something was coming at a most unnaturally fast and ungainly pace – something shapeless, oblong, and whitish.

"It is a tree," Hugh thought confusedly at first. "It is the stump of a silver birch that has been shattered in a gale. With patches of white on its broken trunk, and patches of dark."

And then he thought: "No, it is *not* a tree. It is a person."

And then he thought: "*It is putting itself together as it comes towards me.*"

At this point Hugh let go of his bicycle, which fell on the track, and glanced desperately about him for a stick or stake or some other weapon to fight off the dogs. Go back and confront that whitish, patched-together thing with its long thin arms extended in front of it – that he would *not* do, though Cerberus and all the hounds of hell were lying in wait for him at the farm entrance. In fact he could not even bear to look behind him again and see how close the – whatever it was – had come. Snatching up a crooked piece of oak branch, with a few leaves adhering to it, that had fallen from the hedge, he ran on down the road, stumbling in his terrified haste.

There was no chance of climbing the banks – they were now well above his head, and crowned with dark hedges of thorn or holly.

He could not hear any footsteps of the thing behind him – if it *had* feet – because of the yelling clamour of the dogs ahead.

Now Hugh came to a kind of crossroads where, on either side, gated entrances led to the farm and its outbuildings. The gates hung wide open. To the left, some way back, stood the house – a long, low, shadowy building with numerous dark windows and doors, none of them illuminated.

The whole place was shrouded in dimness and a garden-patch with rows of cabbages and a large well-head lay in front of it. To the right was a spacious farm yard with cart sheds and haystacks, a tumbril, vaguely seen in the twilight, loaded with something that looked like roots, a path of frosted nettles, and a rusty harrow.

What he did see were two men.

They stood on either side of the road, looking at him and at one another, each of them in an open gateway. Their faces were not distinguishable to Hugh in the intense gloom. Here, at the deepest point of the lane, the banks were topped with trees and were twice the height of a man.

Both men stood perfectly still. They did not move. But Hugh received from them such a powerful impression of rage – hate – deadly intent – that it made him tremble. The chill of it was like a knife in his breast.

Words from the Bible came to him: "Their faces shall gather blackness".

"I have *got* to get out of this place, I have got to," he thought, "or I'm done for. Either from them, or from what is behind me. And where is *that*? And do they know it is there?"

He felt himself frozen to the stony ground with terror, and with the fury and malevolence that seemed to be all around him. It seemed to him as if the two men had laid a barricade across the road – a barrier of hate and ill will.

"But they can't *do* that," thought Hugh confusedly. "The road is not theirs. The road is the King's Highway. Nobody is allowed to block it. No body."

No spirit?

He knew himself to be in deadly danger – a danger that he could not understand, that surrounded him like a thick and poisonous smoke.

"If I don't leave this place," he thought, "I shall be shrivelled up like a leaf in a fire. I shall be lost. I am very nearly lost already..."

"I shall fly into fragments like that thing on the road behind me."

He tried to gather himself into a single whole. "I am Hugh Tregear, from Church College

Cambridge, on my way to visit my sister Fanny. I have a lace shawl for her gift, and coral teething-rings with silver bells for the twin babies. I have a book for Tom, my brother-in-law – a book of poems."

"If I could – if I could think of a line from one of the poems..."

Then he thought of a line:

Forth, pilgrim, forth! Forth, beast, out of thy stall...

Hold the high road...

He began to struggle forward, panting, pushing his way with straining muscles and bursting heart through invisible bands of opposition. "They *can't* block the road, they *cannot*, it is the public highway. It is the right of every citizen to walk it unimpeded. Unopposed."

Step by step he forced himself to go forward, with the yelling of the dogs in his ears to right and left. He tried not to look at the two men.

But he was obliged to, for their faces burst into flame. "Their faces shall be as flames," thought Hugh, "all faces shall be burnt therein."

He heard two appalling screams, of hate, rage, despair. But they were behind him.

Then at last Hugh was free and able to run. Sobbing, gasping, crying out, with his heart rattling against his ribs, he pounded onward.

How far he had run or at what point he fell, he did not know, but there came a moment when exhaustion and terror folded over him and he collapsed into a blank and blessed pit of sleep or fainting, which held him numb and close for many hours.

When he next woke he found, to his amazement, that he was in a bed in a small and sunny bedroom. Not far away he could hear the clamour of church bells.

He pushed himself up, exclaiming confusedly, "Where am I? Oh, my heavens, I must hurry –"

"Now don't 'ee fret, my dear, don't 'ee!" soothed a kindly voice. "Reverind Musson, he be over in the church, acelebrating the joyful day, and you being safely preserved; but he'll be back pressingly. Do'ee lie down, now, and take a nice drop of tea, that'll do 'e famous good."

The aproned old lady who spoke now limped out of the room, but returned after a moment, bearing the nice cup of tea and a slice of thin bread-and-butter, which did indeed taste like manna and nectar to our young traveller.

"Where am I?" he asked again.

"Why, you're in the Rectory at Goose Acre, my dear, and Rector hisself he'll tell ye, by and by, all ye want to know. Now just bide ye quiet till he comes."

This Hugh was glad to do. He lay passive in the lumpy hammock-like bed, watching the mild play of flames in the small hearth, and the rooks circling the stone church tower which he could see through the window. And presently the bells, which had gone silent, rang again in a joyful hurricane of final celebration.

Then there came a step on the stair, and a thin, black-haired man with an intelligent, penetrating face, came into the room.

"Mr Tregear?" said this person. "We are so very glad to see you better."

Hugh was astonished. "How did you know my name?"

"Why," he said, smiling, "I took the liberty of examining the papers in your pocket and found the letter from your sister. So then I took the additional liberty of sending her a telegram to inform her that you had suffered a minor accident but were in good hands here, and would be able to join her later on."

"Oh, sir! Thank you!" exclaimed Hugh, immensely relieved. "She will have been so worried. I do feel in good hands – indeed I do! But what happened to me? Where did you find me?"

"You were lucky," said the Rector gravely. "You were wonderfully lucky. We gather that you had suffered a mishap to your bicycle? And so were pushing it, walking along the lane from Cropham, that runs through Rushout Wood and passes the ruin of Oldhouse Farm?"

"Yes – yes – that is what happened." Hugh was puzzled. "The ruin? But surely – ? In any case, how do you know these things?"

"I had been visiting a sick parishioner last night. I was driving back in my motor car. I saw you lying in a heap at Cropham crossroads. So I brought you home, guessing what might have occurred. And this morning Sam Walsingham, one of my farmer parishioners, went out with a haycart and recovered your bicycle. (We deduced the bicycle from the fact that you were wearing trouser clips.) And of course," ended the Rector obscurely, "there is no danger at Oldhouse in daylight."

"Danger? Then –"

"My dear young friend, are you better? Do you find yourself restored enough to rise and share my Christmas meal? I shall be glad to give you the whole explanation, but I believe that you may sustain it better after some solid food. If what my excellent Mrs Rutter has prepared may be so designated."

Hugh exclaimed that he was well, quite well enough to get up, and would be very happy indeed to get up and share the Rector's Christmas lunch.

Eyeing himself in the wash-stand mirror, though, as he shaved, he was quite astonished at the thin, haggard face that looked back at him. It seemed to have aged by seven years since yesterday.

"Now, draw up a chair to the fire," said the Rector, when the festive meal had been despatched, "and I will tell you about the Hernshaw family who lived at Oldhouse Farm a hundred years ago."

"You said ruins just now? Nobody lives there any more? But I heard the dogs barking. And saw two men. And a – and a something –"

"You were fortunate," said the Rector again. "Nobody in this neighbourhood ever walks past Oldhouse Farm at night. In a car, yes, it is safe enough to drive quickly by, or on one of those motor-bicycles. Even perhaps on a bicycle, if one pedalled hard enough and fast enough. But walking is too slow. It lays you open for too long to such terribly malign influences. Especially on Christmas Eve."

"But *why*? What happened there?"

"The farm belonged to a man called Abel Hernshaw, a widower. A surly, sour-natured, ill-conditioned man by all accounts. He had an only son, Mark, who grew up in the course of time, married a girl with some money of her own, and moved to a farm of his own, Cathanger, lying to the west of Rushout Wood. There had been quarrels, tensions between the two men before that, it is said. But all was patched up after Mark moved out; indeed he had a child, Lucy, who was her grandfather's pet by all accounts. A spoiled, wayward little madam, apparently – took after her father and grandfather..."

"Mark with his wife and daughter used to go over to Oldhouse at Christmas time, to spend the day and eat their dinner with the old man."

"It is known that Abel Hernshaw had a hobby of breeding fierce dogs, collies and bull terriers. There would always be two or three about the place, ready to come rushing out and harry any passer-by who took the road that led through the middle of the farm. In the records of the Parish Council there are various notes of complaints against Farmer Hernshaw from people who had been assaulted by his dogs. But his retort always was that nobody was obliged to go that way, through his farm; if they chose they could take the southerly road from Goose Acre to Cropham, which is only a scant half-mile longer."

"That's true," said Hugh, who had noticed this alternative on the map and rejected it.

"Hernshaw said that he was not going to keep his dogs tied up for any man. The job of farm dogs was to run loose and keep guard over the place."

"Well, one Christmas Mark arrived as usual to spend the day with his wife and daughter. But this time he also brought along a dog of his own, just as bad-tempered and combative, it seemed, as those bred by his father. And of course there was a battle between his dog and one of Abel's; a window was broken in the scrimmage, and Abel's dog was hurt so badly that it had to be shot. This made Abel so angry that he told Mark never to come back to Oldhouse again. No more Christmas visits. And during the following year

Abel got himself several more dogs to replace the one that had been killed."

"The next Christmas Lucy demanded to go as usual to her grandfather's. It seemed that he had always hidden a gift for her in the hay barn, and the spoiled child saw no reason why this practice should have been discontinued, just because her father and grandfather had quarrelled. 'What is that to do with me?' she said. 'I want my Christmas toy from grandpapa. It will be in the haymow.' 'He will not have left it this year,' her father told her. 'And I absolutely forbid you to go there.' But Lucy took not the slightest notice of his interdict. She waited until all the household were busy with Christmas preparations, and then put on her mother's Christmas gift to her – a fur coat made from white ferret-skins – and stole away secretly from Cathanger Farm, through Rushout Wood, and so to her grandfather's place. She did not go to the house, but directly to the hay barn where the old man had always hidden her present.

"And, of course, the dogs heard her."

The Rector paused.

"What happened?" asked Hugh with a dry mouth, although he could guess.

"Why, the dogs went after her. She ran. Lucy must have been a fast runner – she had got as far as Rushout Wood when they finally caught up with her. But then they tore her to pieces."

"And her father? And grandfather?"

"Mark Hernshaw went to Oldhouse that evening, as dusk fell, and shot all the dogs. He took lamp-oil with him and set fire to the building and the ricks. The old man came running out and tried to stifle the blaze with brooms and sacks. Nobody else was there; no one would work for him by now. Mark flung oil over his father too, it is thought, and the fire caught him. The two men struggled together, and finally fell, or jumped, into the well. Since that time nobody has lived at Oldhouse Farm."

"What a dreadful tale," said Hugh. "I saw them – it must have been them – on either side of the road, staring at one another. Hating one another."

Of the tattered, dishevelled, leaping thing that had run after him out of Rushout Wood he could not speak.

I suppose, he thought, she comes back to see her grandfather get his just desserts.

"I wonder how long it will go on, the haunting? I felt such an atmosphere of hate – terrible hate."

"When it is as fierce as that I am afraid it may take many more decades, centuries even, to die away," said the Rector sadly. "I repeat that you were lucky, my young friend – supremely lucky – to escape. Some have not been so fortunate. People have been driven out of their wits, or suffered heart attacks. How – can you remember? – how *did* you manage to fight your way through?"

With reluctance, Hugh cast his mind back.

"I think – I was thinking about the road," he said uncertainly. "Thinking that it was every citizen's right to go along it unhindered. And – to wrench my thoughts away from those two figures and their hideous hate – I was going through, in my mind, the presents for my sister and her family that I have in my pack. I thought of a book – yes, the book I had brought for my brother-in-law, and of a poem in it – Chaucer's Ballade of Good Counsel: 'Hold the high road, and let thy ghost thee lead, And Truth thee shall deliver..."

"Ah, now I begin to understand," said the Rector. "And your Guardian Ghost came, very promptly, to the rescue."

"I – I think so," said Hugh. "Yes."

"And the road, perhaps, played its part. Roads are very ancient and powerful constructs – older than buildings, far older than towns, many of them go back unimaginable distances in time. They must in some way hold the essence of all that has been carried along them. They stand for the connection of one spirit to another, the urge to make journeys and discoveries, the need to move in a forward direction, the need to make pilgrimages. Roads, like altars, have rights which must be respected."

"Yes," said Hugh again.

Mr Musson smiled.

"But now you, my young friend, must be on your own road. My neighbour Mr Whinstone the blacksmith has mended your machine. It is only a scant hour from here to your brother-in-law's parish – you will be there long before dark, in time for Christmas tea!"

"Oh, thank you, sir! You have been so kind –"

"No kindness. A great pleasure. And let us hope that, by battling against it so successfully, you may have reduced the malign power of Oldhouse Farm and made that road less perilous for others. Goodbye, and a safe journey to you."

Hugh thanked his host again, shouldered the pack full of presents, and mounting his mended machine, set off pedalling along the flat, straight road that led from Goose Acre to his sister's village. And behind him the westering sun flung out his long shadow, which ran ahead of him along the highway like a beckoning ghost.

READING ZONE!

TOP READING TIP

When reading, it is always a good idea to find a cosy spot where you are comfortable and feel safe.

This is particularly true when you read stories like this that are a quite scary.

If you get a bit nervous you might also want to read them in a nice light and not just before bedtime!

READING ZONE!

WHAT DO YOU THINK?

As well as all being scary stories, there are other links between the stories in this book.

For example, there are several characters who have trouble walking.

Can you think of other examples of things that are similar between the stories?

READING ZONE!

QUIZ TIME

Can you remember the answers
to these questions?

• In *Stoneywish*, who came to look
after Rick when his mum died?

• What do you have to take with you
when you make your Stoneywish?

• In *Snow Horse*, what did Cal carve
from the pile of frozen snow?

• In *Bindweed*, What did Claud do to
Aunt Lily on the night she died?

• In *The Road from Rushout Wood*, why
did Hugh decide not to turn back even
though he was afraid of the dogs?

READING ZONE!

GET CREATIVE

Why not plan and write your own ghost story?

Who will your characters be?

What will your setting be like?

What is going to be the scary thing in your story?

When you have written it, trying telling it to a friend or family member.

Did you manage to scare them?